The girls have a great time singing their favorite songs—really loud!
Suddenly, the doorbell rings.
"Who could that be?" asks Barbie.

Ding-Dong!

Sparkling Microphone Cupcakes

Things you'll need:
Cake mix
A cupcake baking pan
A box of wafer ice cream cones (make sure they have a flat bottom)
Pink frosting
Silver-ball sprinkles

Ask an adult to help you bake the cupcakes, following the instructions on the box. After the cupcakes have cooled, remove them from their wrappers and place each cupcake in an ice cream cone. Frost the cupcakes. Add silver-ball sprinkles on top. Yum!

"You guys are the best," Barbie says to her sisters. "Thanks for turning this gray day into a perfect party!"

"Anything for you," say Skipper, Stacie, and Chelsea. "Happy birthday, Barbie!"

Happy Birthday, Barbie!

Barbie opens the door and finds all of her friends outside. The sisters were having so much fun, they didn't realize that the rainstorm had stopped.

"Happy birthday!" all of Barbie's friends shout.

"Time to decorate the cupcakes!" calls Skipper.

"Look! I made a sparkling microphone cupcake," says Chelsea.

"*You ain't seen* muffin *yet,*" Barbie sings. "*La-la-la.*"

"It's as cute as a cupcake!" exclaims Stacie. "And we can use this pretty pink-and-purple cupcake stand to show off our creations."

Fashion Show Party Tip

You don't need to buy new clothes for a dress-up party. Ask your family and friends if you can borrow some of theirs. Remember to be careful with these borrowed clothes and to return them after your party is over.

The girls decide to clean up and put on their prettiest party dresses for a fashion show.

"Look at me in my puffy party dress!" exclaims Chelsea as she twirls around.

"I'm ready to rock," says Skipper.

Stacie strikes a pose. "Too cool!"

"*Ta-da!*" says Barbie. "Pink is always in style."

Next, the sisters tell Barbie that they all have to get dressed up. But there's one catch: they have to get dressed in each other's closets—in the dark! The person with the funniest look wins!

"*Ahhh!*" All the girls scream and laugh when they see each other in their outfits.

"I think you're the winner, Barbie," Chelsea says, giggling.

"You look so funny!" Chelsea and Stacie squeal as they take off their blindfolds.

"Hello, Fabulous!" Barbie giggles when she looks in the mirror.

"Happy birthday, Barbie!" yell Chelsea and Skipper as they run into Stacie's room.

"Wait until you see our next surprise," continues Stacie. "It's time for the Makeover Madness game!"

The sisters quickly choose teams and do each other's hair and makeup—blindfolded!

"No peeking," says Skipper.

Dazzling Decorations!

Pom-Pom Flowers

1) Stack the colored tissue paper.
2) Fold the paper accordion-style into a fan.
3) Tie the fan in the middle with a piece of string.
4) Round the ends of the paper by cutting them with scissors.
5) Pull the ends of each piece of tissue paper toward the middle to make a pom-pom.
6) Dust with glitter if desired.

Things you'll need:

Colored tissue paper (6–8 full sheets)
String
Scissors
Glitter (optional)

Sensational Streamers

1) With an adult's help, cut the wrapping paper and colored tissue paper into 2-inch-square pieces.
2) Thread a needle with 3 feet of string. Tie a knot at the end.
3) Slide the different pieces of paper onto the string until the streamer is complete.
4) Hang the streamer on the wall.

Things you'll need:

Colorful wrapping paper
Colored tissue paper
Scissors
A needle
String

Happy Birthday!

Chelsea creates pretty pom-poms. Then, with some quick cutting here and a touch of string there, Skipper transforms old wrapping paper into sensational streamers.

"That is so chic!" exclaims Chelsea.

Meanwhile, Skipper and Chelsea race around the house looking for decorations.
"I know! I know!" squeals Chelsea. "Let's make pom-pom flowers!"
"Good idea!" agrees Skipper. "And we can make streamers out of wrapping paper, too."
"They'll be dazzling decorations!" says Chelsea.

Spin-the-Nail-Polish Game

Here's a nail-polish activity to do with your friends. Sit in a cicle and place different bottles of nail polish in the middle. Have the birthday girl spin one of the bottles of nail polish. Whoever the cap is pointing to when it is done spinning must paint one of their fingernails that color. Then that person spins the next color of nail polish, and so on. The girl who has all her nails colored first wins!

"What's this about?" Barbie laughs as she walks into Stacie's room. There are bottles of sparkly nail polish and strawberry lotion, rhinestone-studded nail files, and pretty pink nail stickers everywhere.

"Welcome to the Stylin' Salon!" Stacie greets her. "For your birthday, you'll be pampered from head to toe."

"What a treat for my little feet!" exclaims Barbie. "I love my twinkly toes!"

The sisters send the card to Barbie by special delivery.
"Woof! Woof!" barks Lacey as she runs up to Barbie with the card.

Happy Birthday, Barbie! Go to Stacie's room for the start of your big surprise!

Stacie, Chelsea, and Skipper get right to work on a special invitation for Barbie. They use pictures, buttons, ribbon, hearts, and flowers to make the card perfect.

"Just checked the local weather, and there's a huge thunderstorm blowing through," Skipper announces. "I better text everyone and postpone the party."

"Oh, no!" cries Stacie. "What will we do now?"

"I know!" exclaims Chelsea. "Let's throw Barbie a party right here in the house. We can bake and decorate some sweet treats, play games, and—"

"Sounds like a plan," Skipper says with a laugh. "Let's get this party started—we've got tons to do!"

Suddenly, Stacie notices some dark clouds and raindrops outside.

"Whoa! It looks like it's raining cats and dogs!"

"And bunny rabbits!" Chelsea says, giggling.

"Everyone says they'll meet us at the park at four o'clock. Barbie is going to be so surprised!"

"I love surprises!" squeals Chelsea.

Skipper, Stacie, and Chelsea are so excited. They are throwing a big birthday party for their sister Barbie! Skipper double-checks the guest list.

Barbie

Happy Birthday, Barbie!

By Mary Man-Kong
Illustrated by Kellee Riley

A Random House PICTUREBACK® Book

Random House 🏠 New York

BARBIE and associated trademarks and trade dress are owned by, and used under license from, Mattel.
© 2014 Mattel. All Rights Reserved.
www.barbie.com
Published in the United States by Random House Children's Books, a division of Random House, Inc.,
1745 Broadway, New York, NY 10019, and in Canada by Random House of Canada Limited, Toronto.
ISBN 978-0-385-37320-3
randomhouse.com/kids   MANUFACTURED IN CHINA   10 9 8 7 6 5 4 3